modern**family**

modern family™

Wit and Wisdom from America's Favorite Family

The Writers of *Modern Family*

HYPERION

New York

Family is family. Whether it's the

one you start out with . . . the one that

you end up with . . . or the family

that you gain along the way.

—Gloria

Library of Congress Cataloging-in-Publication Data has been applied for.

ISBN 978-1-4013-2475-9

Hyperion books are available for special promotions and premiums.
For details contact the HarperCollins Special Markets Department in the
New York office at 212-207-7528, fax 212-207-7222, or
email spsales@harpercollins.com.

FIRST EDITION

Designed by Timothy Shaner, nightanddaydesign.biz

1   3   5   7   9   10   8   6   4   2

Contents

Introduction

Welcome to the Family

The year was 2004, and I had a secret.

Yes, I was still at the top of everyone's party list, and yes, I still got plenty of dates (my friend Pepper once said so many people had been in my shower I should have a "Welcome" bath mat). But more and more I found myself thinking about my family back on the farm. Ten years had passed since I'd left home—my dear, sobbing mother saying, "They should put an extra o in 'Missouri' today, because you're putting a hole right in the middle of the state." But now I felt like I was the one with the extra o in his name. *Cameroon*. Like in distant, desolate Africa. That was my dark secret. I was lonely.

Who could imagine that barely six months later, I would be welcomed into one of the most exciting, nurturing, exhilarating families on earth?

I'm talking about the members of the Ninth Street Overpass Acting Society, who generously welcomed me into their gang of performers; renewed my interest in theater and music; let me soar in their production of *No, No, Nanette*; convinced me to give up a safe but unrewarding career as a Brink's guard so I could return to teaching piano; and invited me to one of their fund-raiser dinners, where I daringly asked out one of their patrons—there's your real no-no, Nanette. His name was Mitchell, and the rest, as Pepper would say, is herstory.

Of course I didn't just begin a relationship with Mitchell that day; I began one with his entire family, some of whom took a while warming to me, others of whom took a little longer. That's just the Pritchett way. They're cautious by nature. But I knew that even the heavy fog of Pritchett skepticism was no match for the paisley searchlight that is my personality, and I was right.

I happen to have a mom who is very emotional, but very open and friendly, like a puppy. My dad, on the other hand, is not a warm person, but he's tough and fair and hard when he has to be. I like that about him. So naturally Claire reminded me of my dad and Phil of my mom, and soon we were getting along like a house afire.

Jay, at this time, was still with Dede, which frankly never made sense to me. She seemed like someone who a long time ago had stopped finding the joy in life, and he seemed like someone in a doctor's office, tapping his foot, waiting for someone to tell him something. She finally did tell him what I think he wanted to hear. Off she went to New Mexico, and in came Gloria. It was like love at first sight. I'd never fallen so hard for a woman in my life.

She had style and beauty and attitude—she had *life* in her—and I knew, just knew, that we were meant to be best friends. Except I may have tried a little too hard. The first night we met I remember she said to me, "So what do you think of my two boys? Not too alike, are they?" Like all gay men, I enjoy it when beautiful women talk sassily about their breasts, so I said, "They look pretty alike to me, but now that you mention it, the one on the left might be . . ." That's when I realized she was talking about Jay and Manny.

The kids I have enjoyed since the day I met them. Luke is our mad scientist. Alex is the girl who stares at the phone waiting for her real family to call. And Haley is like me at that age, ready to take the world by storm, just not sure what outfit to wear. Lily and Manny are our philosophers. Not long ago, at a Sunday dinner, Manny was in his latest existential crisis, and he asked the table, "What is happiness?" Lily said, "That's the thing that boys have that girls don't."

It's hard to believe I've only known these people eight years, because I do consider them as much my family now as the people back home. And it's not just because they've accepted me. It's because they've changed me, in a good way, and I've changed them. I can see where I've smoothed some of Jay's harder edges, where Jay has built Phil's confidence, where Phil has helped Manny to remember to have a child-hood, where Manny has helped Haley to feel special—and where we've all helped Gloria not to say "disguise the limit" or "I'm as hungry as a whore is."

I guess that's what I like best about this family I never knew I'd get to have. We make each other better, and we make each other feel a little less alone. So no, Lily, happiness isn't something that boys have. Just the lucky ones. ■

The Dunphys

Sweetheart, I would love to be wrong. I just don't live with the right people for that.

Claire

Your kids don't need
to know who you were
before you had them.
They need to know who
you wish you were, and
try to live up to that
person. They're gonna
fall short, but better they
fall short of the fake you
than the real you.

Motherhood

"If only my mother were here."

How often I've heard myself say those words in my seventeen years navigating the choppy waters of motherhood. "If only my mother were here to show me how not to handle this situation."

It's not that she didn't say positive things. "Well, I just love that top," she would say in a way that let me know how much she hated my pants. Or "You did your best," she'd say consolingly, but always with a little emphasis on the "Your." *Your* best, not other people's best.

And it's not that I blame my mother for sometimes being

disappointed in me. Children disappoint mothers—a lot. I just blame her for not being a better liar about it. Mothers have no excuse for not being better liars because they're surrounded by the best lie instructors on Earth: their children.

Children learn to lie before they learn to talk. It's their first language. And just think of the power they must feel when they first discover it. Imagine a fussy child having his feet forced into the stiff red leggings of the hideous pajamas that Aunt Dottie sent (Aunt Dottie is visiting and the pajamas have been hurriedly yanked from the back of the closet). The child doesn't really care that much. Sure, he'd like to wear the fireman pajamas he usually wears, but let's not get crazy. We're still talking about soft fabric here. So he twists a little, whines a little—he's got to show he's not a pushover—then, just for the hell of it, he lets out a shriek. And what happens? Mom thinks she's sprained his ankle forcing it into the pajamas (which are probably too small), picks him up, showers him with love, and out come the fireman PJs. The child, in that moment, must be filled with more wonderment than Thomas Edison when he saw the first light bulb light up. A simple shriek—a lie—and he not only got the outfit he wanted, but a lot of extra love and attention to boot.

It happens differently for every child, of course. But at some point the lie is discovered and its dark arts are practiced and refined throughout the rest of childhood. So if I have one bit of advice for young mothers it's this: If you think they're lying—if you think there's even a chance they might be lying—they are. ■

Well, honestly, at first, it was hard. I mean, you don't expect to wake up one morning with a new mom who looks like she fell off a mud flap.

But I'm getting used to it, and the important thing is you make him so happy, which you do in, in so many ways . . .

Don't take this the wrong way, but I have almost no faith in you.

What's the plan, Phil?

Oh, Alex, honey, when you're out shopping you might wanna pick yourself up a training bra. I know you don't need it now, but your little boobies are gonna come in soon. Mommy loves you, kitten! Mwah, mwah . . . *(to herself)* teach her to screw with me.

Let me fill you in on a little secret, Luke.

When I met your dad, I was fun, too. But I had to

give all that up, because you can't have two fun

parents. That's a carnival. You know that kid Liam

who wears pajama pants to school and pays for

things with a hundred-dollar bill? Two fun parents.

Mark my words.

Well, you're all wrong.

Because this is incredibly clear

and it's really important. We need

to put these signs up all over the

neighborhood.

Look at them: A minute ago they were

babies, and now they're driving,

and soon we'll all be dead.

*People know you're a girl.
You don't need to prove
it to them.*

Because I have, uh, seen this little show before.
Lying on a bed with a tall senior: One minute
you're just friends, watching *Falcon Crest*, and
the next you're lying underneath the air hockey
table with your bra in your pocket.

*No! No, no. No, no, no. Do
you know what's illegal in
Europe? Nothing. You are
going to college.*

Women in their thirties on the Internet are like ninjas. They get in their little black outfits and try to sneak their way into your marriage.

CLAIRE: Haley, sweetie, wake up.

HALEY: What?

CLAIRE: I need you to teach me to use the TV.

HALEY: Now? Why can't Dad teach you?

CLAIRE: Because we're married.

I have this theory that Phil purposely installs complicated technology so he has a reason to talk to me like I'm a child.

CLAIRE: Because everything is your thing! This . . . this is the one thing that was my thing! This is my only thing! Oh my God, this is my only thing. And then you come along and steal my thunder with your tight dresses and your great ideas. I was the one that all the moms looked up to. I was the only one Gus liked.

GLORIA: Claire, I didn't come here to steal your thunder. Your thunder is your thunder, and my thunder is my thunder!

The first day of school is tough on all my kids. Especially the one I married.

CLAIRE: Phil loves Spandau Ballet. That song "True" was playing in the car the first time we kissed. It's our song. So I did some research and found out the lead guitarist lives like forty miles from here. He was in the phone book. How eighties is that?

PHIL: I've never liked Spandau Ballet. Our entire marriage I've never once mentioned Spandau Ballet. Am I . . . am I even pronouncing that right?

The year was 1991. America was immersed in Desert Storm, meanwhile stateside, another storm was brewing . . . in my heart. This is stupid. After a romantic dinner at Fratelli's, a certain nervous young couple shared their first kiss as the radio played this song.

~~Spandau Ballet "True"~~

Orchestral
Manoeuvres in
the Dark
"If You Leave"

— P

CLAIRE: I was looking through the computers in the house for pornography.

HALEY: Sick.

CLAIRE: Not for me. I wanted to see what you guys were looking at.

HALEY: So you're violating our privacy?

CLAIRE: When I find out that my children are looking at a naked picture online, they don't have any privacy.

ALEX: Who was looking at naked pictures?

CLAIRE: That doesn't matter.

HALEY: I wasn't!

LUKE: It wasn't me! That's gross. I'm ten.

I'm not done, so not done. Look, here's the thing: We . . . we have fireworks at Christmas now because that's what they do in Colombia. I don't mind. Thanksgiving, that used to be me roasting a turkey until the gays took that over with whatever new turkey-cooking craze it is that you saw on the Food Network, and I'm fine with that. All I ask, all I ask, is you leave me Halloween. Yeah, Halloween. I realize that it is a crazy-ass holiday for a grown woman to care about this much, but it's my crazy-ass holiday. Mine.

PHIL: Claire, this is a very delicate situation. If we don't handle it right, Luke might end up having an unhealthy attitude about sex. Or agribusiness. We'll talk about it when he gets home.

CLAIRE: Okay, fine, but I am telling him that every time he looks at porn, God kills a puppy.

PHIL: Maybe I should be the one to talk to him.

CLAIRE: It's two hours of our lives.

PHIL: Fine.

CLAIRE: For our kids.

PHIL: Sometimes I hate the kids.

CLAIRE: I know.

CLAIRE: Come on, Scout. Let go of it. No, no, no, uhhh . . . dog. Look at this!

PHIL: How did he get ahold of your bra?

CLAIRE: Well, uh, we were out on a date. And he has a really nice car, so . . . How do you think? He got it out of the laundry basket! I can't take my eyes off that dog for a second.

Alex! Stop trying to kill your brother. Listen guys, I need your help. We've gotta find your dad one of those iPad thingies. Haley, text everyone you know. Alex? Facebook, chat, tweet, buzz, bling, I don't know. Just do what you have to do.

LUKE: I can't imagine you working.

PHIL: Luke, let me tell you something. That is very offensive to women. Your mom works very hard. It's just now she works for us.

If I say something that everybody else is thinking, does it make me a mean person? Or does it make me a brave person? One who is courageous enough to stand up and say something . . . behind someone's back . . . to a ten-year-old?

CLAIRE: Well, that sounds innocent enough. I mean, drinks with an old girlfriend at an intimate French restaurant?

PHIL: Honey, you're doing that thing where you say what I want you to say but your tone seems mean.

CLAIRE: How come we don't have the same number of containers and lids? Why would they ever get separated?

PHIL: Built-up resentment, money issues, met a younger lid?

MITCHELL: Hey, it's me. What's a good pre-school?

CLAIRE: Uh, well, our kids went to Wagon Wheel.

MITCHELL: And, it was good? You liked it?

CLAIRE: Um, well, my kids are middle-management material at best. We didn't wanna waste a lot of money . . . Yes, Mitchell, it's good.

CLAIRE: Sometimes, I just think my job is to make sure you guys don't fall on your faces.

PHIL: That's a hard job in the Dunphy family. We fall a lot.

CLAIRE: I know.

PHIL: Maybe your real job is to be the person who picks us back up. Nobody does that better than you.

CLAIRE: Honey, do you want any popcorn or anything?

PHIL: No, I'm Good . . . 'n' Plenty. So hold your . . . water 'cause I've got some Twix up my sleeve.

CLAIRE: You may be cool, but I'm . . . wine cooler.

PHIL: I love us.

All week long, I've been telling my girls how to act instead of showing them, but not Phil. Phil could have said, "Alex, relax. Don't take everything so seriously." Or, "Haley, challenge yourself. Don't give up so easily." But instead of talking the talk, Phil walked the walk. And isn't that what we're supposed to do for the people we love? It's definitely a challenge . . . But Phil made it look easy. Seven feet off the ground.

CLAIRE: Oh, gosh. Okay. Gus? Stop scaring Bethenny and fix that light, please. Don't make me come over there.

GUS: I'm busy. You fix it.

CLAIRE: Is this because I said I wouldn't come to the dance with you? Gus, I'm a married woman. People would talk.

GUS: One dance with me, you'd forget all about it.

CLAIRE: Yeah. I already have a husband that doesn't fix lights.

PHIL: She has to run every day or she goes crazy. She's like a border collie.

CLAIRE: You're comparing me to a dog?

PHIL: The smartest dogs in the world.

CLAIRE: What do we do now?

PHIL: Okay, I'm really afraid of reading this situation the wrong way, but I'm eighty percent sure you're coming on to me . . . Okay, now forty.

CLAIRE: We're going to pass into legend. The parents who canceled Christmas.

PHIL: I thought you'd be happy.

CLAIRE: They'll write songs about us, make one of those Christmas specials with those ugly little clay people.

PHIL: Okay, okay, look, don't worry. We're gonna have Christmas. We've raised our kids right. Whoever did it will come forward. Or the other two will rat 'em out.

HALEY: I have a learning disability. The letters jump around on the page and appear backwards.

CLAIRE: Honey, we had you tested like six times. Trust me. I was praying for dyslexia.

Oh, no, no. I haven't seen Mom since . . . let's see . . . oh, she made out with my ex-boyfriend last night.

One long table, honey. If it was good enough for the Last Supper, it's good enough for us.

More than anything, I want my girls to stop fighting and be close. I want them to share clothes and do each other's hair and gossip about boys, like I used to do with Mitchell.

CLAIRE: That's what I do isn't it? I worry. I worry. I think about a tiny little thing and I obsess on it until it's the only thing that I can think about. Oh God, please don't let me screw up our son.

PHIL: Hey, hey, you know why else he's going to be okay? Because somewhere out there is a worried little girl who's making lists and labeling bins and he's gonna find her.

CLAIRE: I don't know. I mean, he makes a point. We don't know the man. And little kids can be friends with old people, right?

PHIL: Of course they can. There's tons of examples: *Up, Gran Torino, True Grit.*

CLAIRE: Cartoon; kills himself; she loses her arm. We gotta go talk to that guy.

Yeah, well, I do want to do some unloading.

I know your type. Life has been bad to you. It

has made you feel small. And then one day,

somebody gives you a fake cop outfit, a toy

badge, and a little SpongeBob tie, and suddenly

it's payback time, right? Well, I got news for you,

Law and Order: Special Parking Unit. Not my fault.

CLAIRE: You know that really dangerous intersection?

PHIL: Where desire meets jealousy, and the result is murder?

Okay, I don't want you to judge me, but I have to say something. Sometimes I wanna punch my kids.

PHIL: I don't like being you.

CLAIRE: Nobody does.

CLAIRE: Oh, since when do you shy away from confrontation, Mr. Tough Talk, Mr. Straight Shooter? Getting a little soft, Grandpa?

JAY: You know, when you get a massage, you sound like a Tijuana prostitute.

DYLAN: I've never been this far from home before.

DYLAN: Now I've never been this far . . .
Now I've never been this far . . .

CLAIRE: Where's a cliff when you need one?

CLAIRE: Girls, let's cool it on the gossip, okay? It's not right, and Carly's got enough problems.

HALEY: What do you mean?

CLAIRE: Well, her mom can't get through soccer practice without a thermos of chardonnay. And don't get me started on the dad. That guy . . . oh!

There may be some bumps along the way,

but we never stop wanting the best for them.

That's what makes it such a tough job . . .

Kinda the best job in the world.

Okay, people. Let's all chillax.

Phil

I guess that's the real circle

of life. Your parents faked

their way through it; you

fake your way through it.

And hopefully you don't

raise a serial killer.

Fatherhood

The video camera shook in my hands. I'd missed the births of my first two children when—in Haley's case because of a Scarsdale diet I was on, in Alex's because of overtraining for a Unicycle Rally to Beat Bulimia—I had fainted in the delivery room. But I was not missing this one. The camera shook, Claire yelled, and suddenly there he was: Luke. And moments later, the nurse took my camera, handed me my son, and shot a video of me staring dreamily out from under that bike helmet at him. It is probably my favorite of the literally thousands of hours of video of myself that I've collected over the years.

What made it so important to me to experience that first moment? It's probably that I didn't want to miss a single milestone of fatherhood, because it's the best job I've ever had. In fact, it's probably a combination of the best parts of all the best jobs I've ever had: the challenge of being a model in a life drawing class in college; the improvisation of being a magician's assistant; the pure adrenaline high of helping an overleveraged young couple find the right no-trapdoor, deferred balloon payment, adjustable rate mortgage after selling them their dream house.

Do I have a favorite moment from fatherhood? That's like asking if I have a favorite child. Of course I do. It was a few years back on Father's Day. The kids had just crawled into bed with us holding their hand-drawn cards and a big tray of pancakes, Claire had just slipped off to the closet to get her disappointing gift, and the phone rang. It was my dad, who'd just opened the metal detector I'd sent him. I was happy. And suddenly it occurred to me that Luke wasn't all that far from the time he might be enjoying Father's Day himself. And suddenly I had a glorious vision from the future: me, my dad, and Luke, all calling each other, probably live talking on our TV walls—three generations of Dunphy fathers surrounded by kids and presents and pancakes and syrup—and I thought, "What a wonderful world that will be." ∎

CLAIRE: Hmm, so you can say you are a . . . national man of mystery.

PHIL: Shh, I never did catch what you do.

CLAIRE: Didn't you?

PHIL: Surprising, I know. I'm usually pretty good at catching things from women in bars.

I'm the cool dad. That's . . . that's my thing.

I'm hip. I . . . I surf the web. I text: LOL,

laugh out loud; OMG, oh my God; WTF,

why the face. I know all the dances to

High School Musical, so . . .

Hey! Daddy in the hiz-house.

It's like that. You just . . . you just stare down at them. Let the eyes do the work. You might be saying, "Hey, we cool," but your eyes are saying, "No, we not." *(Points to mouth.)* "Nice to meet you." *(Points to eyes.)* "No, it's not." *(Points to mouth.)* "S'all good." *(Points to eyes.)* "S'no it . . . s'nistn't."

I CAN'T BE SATISFIED

CALL ME!
310-555-0167

CLAIRE: "I can't be satisfied"? My God, Phil. That makes me look like a prostitute.

I love you when you're human.

You look hot enough to cook a pizza on . . . in.

You're all the porn I need.

I've always said that if my son thinks of me as one of his . . . idiot friends, then I've succeeded as a dad. If he wants to go the wrong way on the escalator, I'm on board. If he wants to go into a restaurant and pretend we're Australian, then g'day, mate. Toss a few shrimp on the barbie for me and my joey. Yeah, right?

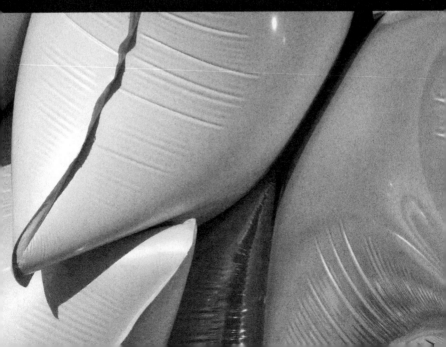

I called the florist and ordered one dozen Mylar balloons. Good luck staying mad, honey.

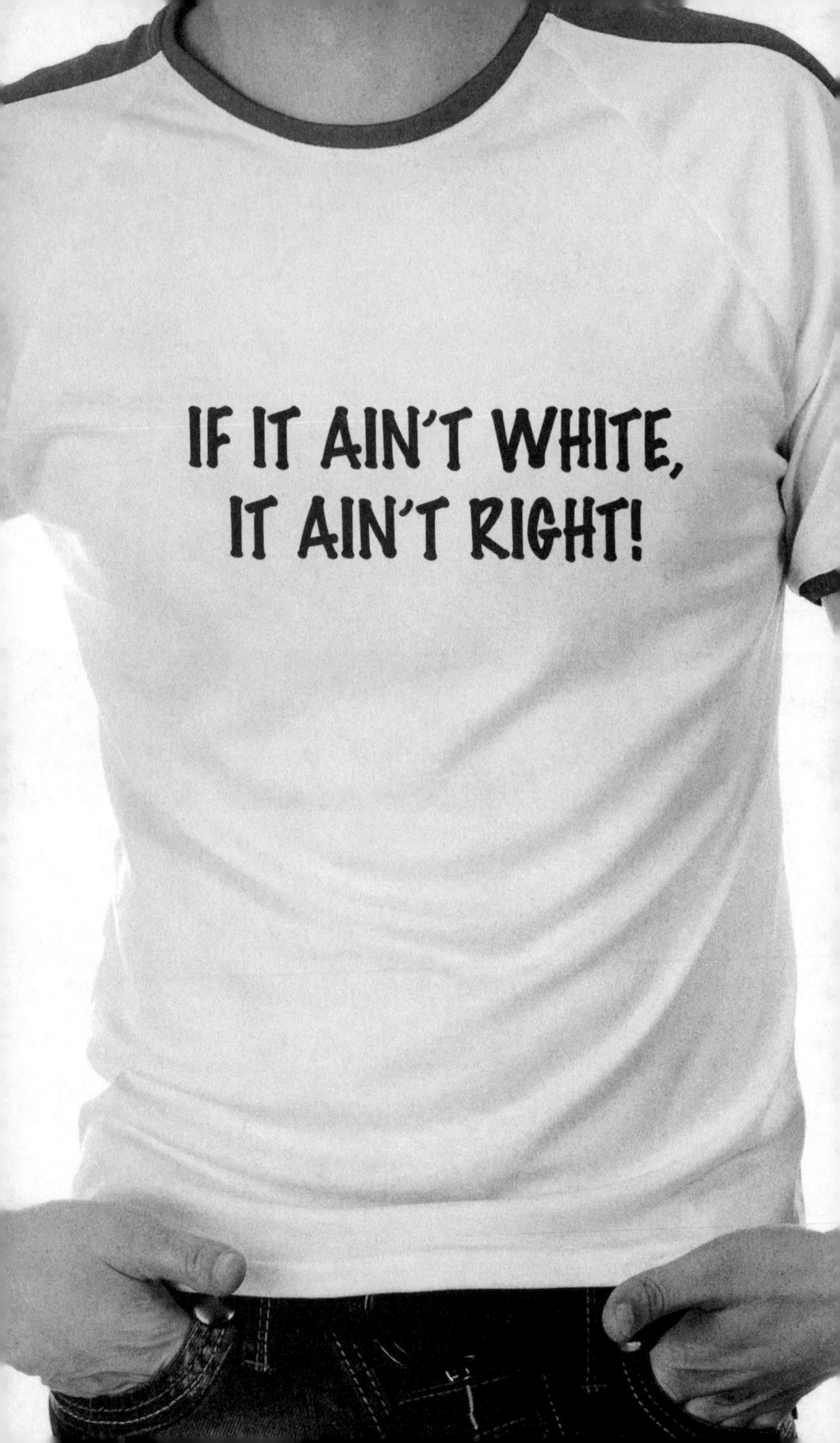
IF IT AIN'T WHITE,
IT AIN'T RIGHT!

PHIL: She was on team blue or, as I like to refer to them, as team blue-ser. And I was on white.

CLAIRE: That's good.

PHIL: And if you ain't white, you ain't right!

CLAIRE: Phil, have you learned nothing?

We're not going to play good cop/mom.

Well, the first day of school can be tough for stay-at-home moms. Now, you have to understand: The kids are gone. The nest is empty. They are rudderless. And a lot of guys wouldn't even notice, but I'm not a lot of guys. I listen, with my mind. And, if you pay attention, women will tell you what they want, by telling you the opposite of what they want. Like the other day, Claire was like, "You have to move your car. There's no space in the garage for both of our cars." And what she's really saying is that, you know, I should probably get a sports car.

I mean, am I attracted to her? Yes.

Would I ever act on it? No. No way.

Not while my wife is still alive.

I've got Gloria!

HALEY: Eww. Dad, is there something you want?

PHIL: Yes, there is. To connect with this girl right here. Now, come on, pretend I'm not your dad. We're just a couple of friends kickin' it in a juice bar.

HALEY: What's a juice bar?

PHIL: Okay, a malt shop, whatever . . .

HALEY: Dad, I don't—

PHIL: No. Who's Dad? Who's Dad? I'm . . . I'm Marcus from biology. Hey, Haley how's it going with you and Dylan? Has he tried anything inappropriate with you? Girl.

PHIL: Hey, coupons for . . . five free hugs.

CLAIRE: You don't like it.

PHIL: Are you kidding me? I love it. It's so . . . creative. Coupons for hugs, which are usually free, but this makes it official, which is so great.

Um, things I want: robot dog, night-vision goggles, bug vacuum, GPS watch, speakers that look like rocks . . . I love my wife, but she sucks at giving gifts. I'm sorry for the pay-channel language, but . . . oh, yogurt maker. I can't not think of things I want.

PHIL: Every year, Luke's birthday falls right around Thanksgiving and so it gets lost in the holiday shuffle.

CLAIRE: Yeah, one year we forgot completely and we had to improvise a cake out of stuffing.

PHIL: Which, by the way, he was fine with. He's one of those you get him a gift and all he wants to do is play with the box.

CLAIRE: Yeah, one year we actually just got him a box. A really nice box.

PHIL: And we made the mistake of putting it in a gift bag.

CLAIRE: So he played with the gift bag.

PHIL: We can't get it right.

Jay and I are "buds" for sure. But with kind of
an invisible asterisk. Um, he's not the . . . he's not
a talker. Or . . . or a hugger. Once he ran over
my foot with his car. To . . . to be fair, he had just
given up smoking. But, basically, we're buds.

CLAIRE: Yeah, a crafts table. You know, everybody gathers around and they make stuff. And then bam! They've got their own party favor.

PHIL: Sorry, I fell asleep while you were describing the most boring party ever.

PHIL: No, no. No, no, no. I want the most dangerous reptile you've got.

TANYA: I have an iguana that, uh, eats crickets.

PHIL: That would be scary if it was a birthday party for crickets, but seriously, Jungle Tanya, I need you to step it up a notch. Is there anything that scares the cocoa out of you?

I am brave. Roller coasters? Love 'em. Scary movies? I've seen *Ghostbusters* like seven times. I regularly drive through neighborhoods that have only recently been gentrified.

CLAIRE: This is unacceptable and I wanna know who did this. Hmm?

PHIL: Nobody, huh? I guess the couch did it to itself. I guess it came home after a tough day, lit up a cigarette, and then it burned itself. Is that what happened? Because that makes no sense.

The firemen in our town have a reputation for being . . . hot. Do I resent it? Of course not, these guys are my friends. I've played basketball with them. I've baked for them. My question is: What's hot?

No, by all means, Claire, we want you looking your sexiest when the hunky gay firemen get here!

We don't know that. It's a miracle I'm standing up. But look, in case anything happens, I want you to know that if I'd had time, I woulda fixed that step.

That was hardly porn. It was a topless woman on a tractor. You know what they call that in Europe? A cereal commercial.

PHIL: I got this. I was his age once. Breasts are these scary, mystical things that he's drawn to like Frodo to Mordor.

CLAIRE: Okay, I'm definitely going—

PHIL: Boys don't want their moms talking to them about sex any more than girls want their dads talking to them about periods, bras, and girdles and all that stuff.

CLAIRE: You do know that women stopped wearing girdles like thirty years ago?

PHIL: Honey, I know. I know. That . . . that, that is exactly the kind of sexual revolution that our son is going through right now. So, just, let's just . . . just trust it.

It must be so hard being a single mom. Claire,
if you want to fly, I'm not going to hold your
feet to the ground. I want to be the one to
push you off the cliff.

PHIL: I'm telling you, you are gonna love this bad
boy. You know what can't climb trees?

LUKE: Raccoons?

PHIL: Worries. Raccoons can and will get up here,
so don't leave any food, or they'll get territorial and
attack.

I'll admit it . . . I'm turned on by powerful women. Michelle Obama, Oprah, Condoleezza Rice, Serena Williams. Wait a minute.

LUKE: You had a girlfriend before Mom?

PHIL: Try two. Trust me, I had plenty of fun in my time. And then I met your mom.

PHIL: Quick, who sang "Evil Woman"?

MITCHELL: What?

PHIL [*answers phone*]: *ELO.*

Why do I have to watch a French movie? I didn't do anything wrong.

What's my coaching philosophy?
Give a kid a bird . . . and he becomes one of
those weird dudes who walks around with a
bird on his shoulder. But give him a pair of wings,
and he can fly . . . unless he has absolutely
no hand-eye coordination.

Next week? That's like the
worst thing you can say to
an early adopter.

PHIL: I don't know. My idea was to have the whole family in a giant bed like in *Willy Wonka*.

CLAIRE: But that's ridiculous.

PHIL: Ridiculicious.

CLAIRE: We didn't even have a proper wedding. We just went down to the courthouse on a Tuesday.

PHIL: The judge sentenced me to life with no chance of parole.

Whoa, whoa, whoa . . . what's the hot topic on *The View* today, ladies?

Okay, here's the thing. I wasn't pushing. In fact, I was pulling a little. It dawned on me that as long as Claire was stuck in the bathroom I'd have time to anchor the cabinet to the wall. It's like they say: Sometimes when God closes a door, he does it so hard that your wife can't get out.

CLAIRE: Boy, I wish Haley would date some other boys.

PHIL: What's that you say, Mrs. Robinson?

Here's a little trick that I've found pretty useful with Claire: "The computer and the printer must talk, talk, talk. Command p makes the picture walk, walk, walk."

The art of the sale is all about what you leave out.

Eighty-three classic wagon . . . *tough to find parts.* They don't make them like this anymore . . . *for legal reasons.* Enjoyed for many years by one happy family . . . *of raccoons.*

I'm kidding.

PHIL: Claire, I know you've got your methods, but so do I. And I'm sorry, but I'm not a micromanager. Trust me. I can provide Luke with the tools and guidance he needs without, uh, smothering him.

CLAIRE: You think I smother our child?

PHIL: It's not your fault, honey. Mother is part of the word. You never hear of anyone being sfathered to death

PHIL: I remember the speech that won me treasurer of my high school Spanish club. *"Mi nombre es Felipe. Yo voy a la escuela . . ."*

CLAIRE: Felipe.

PHIL: It was kind of a *grande* deal. I was up against an actual Puerto Rican.

Halfway through the dinner, I told Claire that whenever she had the urge to lash out at her mother, she should just squeeze my hand instead. A doctor had to cut off my wedding ring.

You can't unplug
my funny bone.

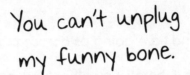

Happy Valenbirthaversary?

Holy crap, we've been
Shawshanked.

Guys, I am just bursting with pride right now. Your

first dance. Soon you're gonna be men. I want

you to know that there's more to being a man

than just shopping for fancy outfits.

Claire and I are going as corpse bride and groom. As if there's any other kind, am I right? I'm saying that marriage kills you.

Bring it, Laura. You wanna test me? I've been tested my whole life. They could never find anything.

I wish I were one of those people who thrives on the danger of leading a double life. You know, Bruce Wayne, Peter Parker, Hannah Montana . . .

PHIL: Yeah, our kids walked in on us. We were, as they say, "having sex."

CLAIRE: That's not a euphemism, Phil. It's exactly what we were doing. Having sex . . . in front of our children.

PHIL: Well, they weren't there when we started.

CLAIRE: No.

PHIL: In fact, you weren't even there when we started.

"Guys, I can't go to Vegas because my wife's freaking out." Trust me, that is not a phone call you wanna make to a bunch of ex-college male cheerleaders. They will mock you with a hurtful rhythmic taunt.

ALEX: Why is he taping our laptop shut?

HALEY: Because he's out of his mind.

They're monsters, Claire, deceitful, manipulative monsters and they need to be broken.

No more lies! You poked the bear, girls! You poked him!

Look, your whole life, my job's been to protect

you. A job I kind of love. And I feel like I'm

being forced into early retirement. I just

needed to find you and make sure you were

okay. For as long as I still get to do that.

CLAIRE: Okay, let's see. Oh, can you grab me an extra virgin—

PHIL: I think one's enough for the sacrifice.

CLAIRE: Olive oil, Phil.

PHIL: Oh, that's funny.

CLAIRE: It's funnier than your freestyle "sandwich rap."

PHIL: Girl, you're crazy. I'm mad fun to shop with. Trapped in between two whole wheat slices. Pastrami and swiss are my only vices.

Busy day at the Dunphy compound . . . We have a wedding tonight, and this afternoon, Claire is debating Duane Bailey in the race for town council. And now the *Weekly Saver* says that some voters find Claire, quote, "angry and unlikable." To those voters I say, "Wait till she sees this."

PHIL: Ladies and gentlemen, I've lived with this woman for twenty years.

CLAIRE: Mm-hmm.

PHIL: If she wants a stop sign, there's gonna be a stop sign.

PHIL: If I had a son, I'd want him to be like Kenneth Ploufe.

CLAIRE: You do have a son.

PHIL: I am Phil Dunphy, and I am not a pervert. I, like a lot of men in this town, enjoy making love to my wife. I mean, uh, I mean with their wives. Not me, them. Look, I should probably just sit down and say nothing, but it's too late. I am standing, and I'm obviously talking, and now you're looking at me, and I feel the need to keep going. First of all, no charges were filed. Everyone had a good laugh . . . about the situation . . . not . . . not about me. Everything's fine down there. Anywho. Where were we?

CLAIRE: All over YouTube. We went viral.

PHIL: Some sick bastard Auto-Tuned me.

CLAIRE: I can assure you; you are perfectly fine.

PHIL: That's very comforting coming from a marketing major at a party school.

Everybody's afraid of something, right?
Heights, clowns, tight spaces. Those are things
you get over. Will they be safe? Those are fears
you never get past. So, sometimes all you can
do is take a deep breath, pull them close,
and hope for the best.

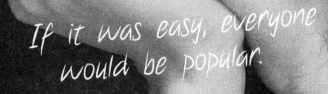
If it was easy, everyone would be popular.

Haley

Why are you guys yelling

at us when we're way

upstairs? Just text me.

Teenagers

I have always been old for my age.

What I mean by this is, the things that interested other fourteen-year-old girls, such as the latest boy band or must-have hair product, would not have interested me when I was fourteen because they would have interested me when I was thirteen and I would have been bored with them by then.

I do not say this to say that I am cooler than other girls, just that I may see trends before they do.

When our entire school started going to Freedom to Juice on Atlantic Boulevard, Gwen Michaelman saw me walk in one day and said, "Oh, look who finally heard about this place."

It was one of the supreme delights of my life to pull the Freedom to Juice punch card out of my pocket, show her the *nine* punches I already had, and watch her face turn the color of a Kale Cleanse.

Of course I am not sure where this will lead in life. Perhaps to a career in fashion, in France. But I did learn one thing in high school (that's right, Mom!) and that is that everyone is insecure about who they are, so you might as well be yourself. I learned this during one very bad day when all of my teachers were stressing me out, I'd just broken up with my boyfriends, my skin was a disaster, and I really just needed to have a good outfit day. So I wore a cute cowboy top, my best jeans, and some white Uggs I'd just gotten.

Halfway to school, my moronic brother dropped a huge glob of jelly from his toast right on the ankle of my white boot. But I didn't panic. I took the bandanna I had in my hair, tied it around my ankle, and walked in. And the next day I saw two freshman girls wearing bandannas on their ankles.

My dad used to tell us, "There are followers in this world, and there are leaders, but if you don't have both kinds you can't have a game of Follow the Leader." How right he was. ∎

ALEX: Did you draw on my poster?

HALEY: Yeah, I did. Maybe you'll think about that the next time you read my journal.

ALEX: I didn't read your stupid journal, and I waited in line to get this signed, Haley.

HALEY: Oh, don't be such a baby. It's just some dude with weird hair.

ALEX: That's Maya Angelou, idiot.

HALEY: Ooh, sorry I don't follow the WNBA.

◼

I thought I IM'ed you to stay away.

HALEY: Shut up and let me help you. The world is divided into two groups. Cool girls . . . and girls like you. And you have been given a rare opportunity to move from the former to the latter.

ALEX: The latter to the former.

HALEY: Whatever. Oh my God, you're such a geek! Now, do you want to be smart or do you want to be popular?

If another woman is messing with your man, you have to get proactive. I don't care how pretty she is, or how many stupid reptiles she has; she tries to take what's mine, girlfriend's gonna get stung.

HALEY: Can I have forty dollars for lunch?

CLAIRE: Forty dollars?

HALEY: I also need a book for school.

CLAIRE: What book?

HALEY: I want a dress.

CLAIRE: Do you have any idea what a bad liar you are?

ALEX: I'd be more worried that she couldn't come up with a single book title.

CLAIRE: But you are really lucky that this did not end as badly as it could've. This is why we always say to you, "When you drink, you make bad decisions."

HALEY: I know. I know. I just . . .

CLAIRE: One minute you're having wine coolers at homecoming and next, the game of "Truth or Claire" sweeps your high school.

HALEY: Thanks for not yelling at me.

CLAIRE: Honey, that would just be cruel. I'll wait till you feel better to yell.

HALEY: I don't think I'll ever feel better. Does this happen every time you drink?

CLAIRE: Yes, yes, it does.

The stars are falling from the sky
And you're the reason why
The moon is shining on your face
'Cause it finally feels it's found its place.
'Cause baby I just want to do you
Do you
Do you want to do me do me?
Underneath the moonlight
Moonlight
Baby maybe, I'll just steal you
Just so I can feel you
Maybe that would heal you
Heal you on the inside.

Oh, I know Mackenzie . . . cute, popular . . . I am Mackenzie. I invented Mackenzie. And the way she's making my sister run around, it's kinda, it's kinda funny, but I can't have it. It's bad for the family.

DYLAN: But I love you!

HALEY: Well, you should have thought about that before you took that skank Sharon Nicolini to an Anne Hathaway movie!

DYLAN: I didn't take her. She was just there.

HALEY: Oh, you were just there by yourself at an Anne Hathaway movie? I don't think so.

DYLAN: Yeah. Yeah. I like her movies. She's everywoman. Come on. Let's not fight. Let's just discuss this like two unimmature adults.

CLAIRE: So, I am your mother and it is my job to make sure that you girls don't get involved with a predator.

HALEY: Okay, Mom, stop watching *Dateline*!

HALEY: Check it . . . I'm a scary black cat.

CLAIRE: The only person that costume scares is me. Go change it.

GLORIA: Taxi! You see? They don't stop because I'm Latina.

HALEY: Or because that was just a yellow car.

I haven't been single
since I was nine.

PHIL: You know I love your mother, but I think you also know a certain look she gets that says, "Just listen to me. I'm always right."

HALEY: You mean her face?

HALEY: I won't be home till late. I have another shift at the restaurant.

PHIL: That's our working girl. Let the river run, honey.

ALEX: It's our parents' anniversary so we're surprising them with breakfast in bed.

HALEY: They're impossible to buy for. We think. We've never really tried.

ALEX: Don't even think about it.

LUKE: But she's sad.

HALEY: Sad she's losing. She just hit you with her best shot. We need to stay strong.

LUKE: But I feel—

HALEY: Don't feel! Just go splash water on your face and man up! We're your mother now!

I'm not saying I miss Dylan, but at least he was romantic. David never sent me a jar of his own tears.

ALEX: This is a mistake.

GABBY: Why does she keep saying that?

HALEY: Because they're the first words she ever heard.

God, I miss you, too. Oh, it's just a
cold, silly. You don't have to conceive
of a world without me . . . Oh,
nothing. I'm just in bed with my mom.
. . . Stop freaking out. It is not
coming true.

My mom's not dumb. You can't just ask her to do something for you. You have to very carefully put the cheese in the trap.

CAMERON: Okay, so, the numbers are by the phone. There's food in the fridge. I just changed her diaper, so all you need to do is put her down in about half an hour and not let a serial killer in the front door.

HALEY: Well, what if he's cute?

MITCHELL: Well, then save him for us.

HALEY: If you do this you'll be a social piranha!

ALEX: Yes, I'll be an Amazonian carnivorous fish.

ALEX: I like the way I dress.

HALEY: Uncle Cam, as her future prom date, would you please talk to her? You know fashion.

CLAIRE: Are those Haley's scores? Are you sure?

HALEY: Why? Are they bad?

CLAIRE: No. They're not bad.

HALEY: Are they good?

CLAIRE: No, they're average. Sweetie, we did it. Our baby's average.

PHIL: Medium-five!

I need to get started on my college essay. You know what? Maybe it'll be about you. You're just so inspirational. Girl power. You rock.

CLAIRE: Oh my God, what are you doing here, girls?

ALEX: Well, we went door-to-door, and we got you twenty more signatures.

CLAIRE: That is so sweet of you.

HALEY: Well, you were freaking out about it, so . . .

CLAIRE: Okay. You know, let's not ruin it.

HALEY: Take a breather. It's just a dent. And saying nothing is not lying, okay? It's just letting the truth speak for itself.

ALEX: This is not the time for moral equivocation.

HALEY: Okay, I don't know what that means. And also, don't tell me.

ALEX: Listen to you. Are you going to be a career criminal?

HALEY: Oh, you sound like Mom. I don't know what I'm going to do after high school.

HALEY: "What's the biggest obstacle you've ever had to overcome?" Didn't my third-grade teacher say I had like ADD or something?

CLAIRE: Oh, no, honey. She said you couldn't A-D-D, and she put it that way because she also knew you couldn't S-P-E-L-L.

Why do I even need to learn Spanish? I live in California. I'm never gonna use it.

CLAIRE: Why are you so frustrated?

HALEY: Because I've never had any obstacles to overcome.

CLAIRE: Oh, honey, that's not true.

HALEY: Really? Name one.

CLAIRE: Well . . . you're lactose intolerant.

HALEY: Oh. "Dear College, cheese makes me gassy. See you in September."

CLAIRE: Sweetie, you're not really starting your essays "Dear College," are you?

Alex

You're never alone when you have books.

No offense, but the

family's hopes and

dreams are kind of

pinned on me.

School

I had gone to my school counselor.

"A strange, depressed feeling comes over me once a week," I told her. "And it's always on the same day, this sense of dread that the fun part of the week is over and the drudgery part is about to start."

"Relax," she told me. "Most kids feel that."

Most kids? I was elated. I don't get to be "most kids" very often.

"Really?" I said. "Most kids get depressed on Friday afternoon because the school week is over?" That's when she asked the other counselor to come in.

I can't help it. I've always loved school. I like learning. I like challenge. You don't learn to play the cello before you can even hold it up for any other reason. Oh sure, people might say it's all because I'm a middle child. That I never got as much attention as adorable Haley, or precious Luke, so I've got to push myself just so I'll stand out. I find that a little insulting.

See, some of us just like the life of the mind. Not everyone is obsessed with getting attention. Maybe some of us just like mastering subjects and honing abilities. Maybe some of us just like the idea of being an all-county debater/science fair winner/lacrosse goalie/junior-congress delegate/straight-A student because, sure, a lot of people have some of these skills. But not many people have all of them. No they don't. Not many at all. ■

ALEX: What's Jägermeister?

PHIL: Um, well, you know how in a fairy tale there's always a potion that makes the princess fall asleep, and then the guy starts kissing her? Well, this is like that except you don't wake up in a castle; you wake up in a frat house with a bad reputation.

◆

Even the advice I get is a hand-me-down.

Oh, my God, welcome

to my world. Last week, I

got this beautiful plaque

from the debate team for

outstanding achievement,

and what did my mom

do? She found one

of Luke's "participant"

ribbons and a certificate

Haley got for showing

up somewhere on time,

and put all three of them

together on the same

shelf. It's like so unfair.

HALEY: Sitting all by yourself at the table. Now, where have I seen that again? Oh, right. Every day in the school cafeteria.

ALEX: I do that by choice.

HALEY: The school's choice.

ALEX: Isn't that your nickname?

CLAIRE: Haley, be nice to your sister. Alex, good save.

ALEX: Could you *L* a little less *O-L*? Don't you see what I'm trying to do here?

HALEY: Die alone?

I didn't want to ruin their moment by telling them how many awards I've gotten, but let's just say I don't get out of bed for a trophy that size.

HALEY: Well, have you guys kissed yet?

ALEX: No!

HALEY: What are you waiting for?

ALEX: I'm not waiting. I'm thirteen.

HALEY: And you've never kissed a boy?

ALEX: How old were you?

HALEY: Like, eleven. And it was beautiful. I was in Jackson Kaner's carpeted garage.

Wait, don't talk yet. Here's the thing.

We've been texting for a while

and it's been nice, but I feel like

it's leading to something else, and

I don't know if you do or not, but I

guess what I'm trying to say is, I'm

just a girl standing in front of a boy

asking for him to like her. Oh God,

that's from *Notting Hill*, so dorky, but

a really underrated movie.

GLORIA: Why you don't wanna wear a dress?

ALEX: Because I don't want to look like Haley and her stupid friends.

GLORIA: I wear dresses and I don't look like Haley.

ALEX: You are Haley, just forty years older.

GLORIA: Ten.

ALEX: Twenty.

GLORIA: Deal.

ALEX: What's the difference between a gamete and a zygote?

PHIL: Don't fall for it, Claire. She's just making up words.

◆

CLAIRE: How did you get so smart?

ALEX: I've always assumed adoption or baby switch.

◆

ALEX: So dumb guys go for dumb girls, and smart guys go for dumb girls? What do the smart girls get?

PHIL: Cats mostly.

It's ironic that I stand up here representing my classmates when for the past three years, most of them have treated me like I'm invisible. It's my own fault... I was obsessed with good grades instead of looks, popularity, and skinny jeans.

It's ironic that I stand up here representing my classmates when... they're so awesome they should be up here themselves. But I'm up here... and I'm saying stuff... 'cause everybody's got their stuff. Whether you're popular or a drama geek... or a cheerleader... or even a nerd like me, we all have our insecurities. We're all just trying to figure out who we are. I guess what I'm trying to say is... don't stop believin'. Get this party started.

HALEY: Okay, Mom, you cannot have a problem with this. I'm Mother Teresa.

CLAIRE: Are you kidding me?

HALEY: What, I'm her back when she was hot.

CLAIRE: I will pay you ten dollars to go put on more clothes.

ALEX: Bet it's the first time you've ever heard that.

◆

HALEY: Okay, fine. Then I will just go put on your favorite nerdy T-shirt. The one with the guy from *Back to the Future* on it!

ALEX: That's Albert Einstein! And it is not nerdy!

Book? Wake up and smell the Internet, Grandma.

Luke

Sometimes I just say, "Are you, Dad? Are you?" Because he gets real quiet and doesn't notice when I walk away.

Siblings

Mr. Ban Ki-moon,
United Nations

Dear Mr. Ki-moon,

Hate is a strong word. I dislike my sisters.

I am not saying this because at times they have dressed me up like a girl and called me Betty Luke. Or because they have filled my house with so much perfume in the morning that I have left for school smelling like a Louisiana prostitute.

I am also not referring to the many times they have jacked my iPod, eaten yogurts clearly marked with my name, "lost" the remote when it was my turn to control it so I was forced to watch shows about girls they think they are hotter than but that are way hotter than them, or destroyed my concentration on my studies with their so-called "music."

No, I am referring to their moods.

Imagine a household where at any moment there could be:

1. Sobbing (boyfriend didn't call)

2. Screaming (got answer wrong, going to get "A-" on test)

3. Shrieking (heard latest gossip)

4. More sobbing (girls at school said she looked fat in those jeans—
   should have thought of that before eating every yogurt in sight)

And these moods invade the whole house. You feel them when you walk in the front door. It's like when I go to my friend Theodorous Koufos's house and I smell the strange cooking halfway up the front step. It makes you not want to go on.

I have spoken to my parents about the problem, but I thought a letter from you might help. I have also written to The Hague in the Netherlands. Please remember that the only thing needed for bad people to get their way in the world is for good people to do nothing.

And I would like a dog.

Yours sincerely,
Luke Dunphy

ALEX: What's the most irritating thing my parents say to me?

MANNY: "That's too much cologne."

HALEY: "That's how girls end up dead."

LUKE: "Don't talk black to me."

MANNY: "It's inappropriate because she's your teacher."

LUKE: How do you even talk black? End words with "izzle"?

ALEX: It's talk back, you idiot.

LUKE: Oh.

I'm not an idiot. I knew what they were up to. But I've been wanting to move for a while. There's a line of ants going to a trick-or-treat bag in my closet, and I don't want to still be there when they get tired of candy.

LUKE: So what was the picture of?

PHIL: Well, it was a woman on a tractor and she had her shirt off.

LUKE: Was it hot?

PHIL: Okay, we're being honest here. Um, this particular woman . . . well, my tastes do run to the curvy, and the cowboy hat did not hurt one bit. Couple that with the cutoff jeans . . . and you were asking about the weather, weren't you?

LUKE: Yeah.

LUKE: I broke the glass

coffee table.

PHIL: The one you swore

you didn't break . . .

and then we blamed

Esperanza and fired her

and she stole a turkey at

Thanksgiving for her family

and got deported?

LUKE: I made fun of him because his mom used to dig coal.

GLORIA: What?

MANNY: He said you were a coal digger.

PHIL: Okay, I think we can move on.

GLORIA: Who said I was a "coal digger"?

LUKE: That's what my mom told me.

ALEX: What's a coal digger?

PHIL: Sweetheart, you heard it wrong. It's gold digger.

CLAIRE: Well, I really do not think I remember ever saying that.

LUKE: Well, you said it in the car; you said it at Christmas; you said it at that Mexican restaurant—

CLAIRE: Okay. Mister leaves-his-sweatshirts-at-school-every-day suddenly remembers everything. Thank you.

PHIL [*on speakerphone*]: Hey, I just wanted to tell you how great you were last night.

CLAIRE: Uh, Phil—

PHIL: Sorry I got the oil everywhere. But hey, they're not our sheets, right?

CLAIRE: Sweetie, honey, honey, remember when the salesman told us that the Sienna was built with the whole family in mind?

PHIL: Yeah . . .

CLAIRE: Uh, well, the whole family just heard that.

PHIL: Well, I . . . guess . . . I guess the Bluetooth works.

CLAIRE: Hmm.

LUKE: Why did you have oil?

PHIL: Because . . . buddy, we were making french fries.

There's no fire escapes! They cut corners!

I'll cut your corners!

LUKE: You do fun stuff. You put that potato chip in my sandwich. That was a crunchy surprise.

CLAIRE: No, that was your dad. Everything fun is your dad. Second Christmas, Italian accent night, this race.

○

CLAIRE: Luke, honey, come back. I said I was sorry.

LUKE: I'm twelve. I need limits!

LUKE: I don't think Grandpa's having the best time. He keeps going and getting more drinks.

HALEY: Well, not every time. One time he went in to check the women's basketball score.

The other day, Uncle Mitchell brought over a bag of junk food so he and Cam could do a Jew fast.

The Pritchetts

Jay

There's nothing mystical about an earthquake. Pressure builds, and it's released. But it makes us realize what matters, and for me that's family. My family. And golf.

I wasn't the greatest husband the first time around. But I'm trying to do a better job this time. And maybe by my third marriage, I'll have it down pat.

Marriage

I've always believed that pain is the best teacher.

Sure, your parents can tell you six ways to Sunday not to touch a hot stove, but it's just words until you yank your hand away from that metal burner. And that blister is your diploma. You will never have to be educated again about the danger of the stove.

So why are people such bad learners? Because they always think one thing: It will be different for me. My grandfather told me about a freezing February afternoon he spent with his tongue stuck to a lamppost that some older kids had tricked him into licking. "Don't ever do that," he said. "Okay," I said. But what I thought was: "What if I just do it a little? Maybe it will be different for me." Well, I'll never get back the four hours I spent stuck to the bumper of my father's Impala before a neighbor came outside with a pan of warm water, and I'll never get back the patch of skin I lost either. I still pronounce "*th*" funny. "*Th*" like in "think."

So why, you might ask, after the pain I had in my first marriage, would I lick the bumper a second time? Because, I realized, it's not our brains that say, "It's going to be different this time." It's our hearts. The brain can say, "The odds are all against this. I've got pages of statistics that say what a bad idea this is, that there isn't a shred of logic to what you're doing, that this *isn't* going to work out." And the heart says, "But what a story it will be if it does." And the heart wins every time.

That's my best guess anyway. And it doesn't hurt when the bumper looks like Gloria's. ■

JAY: Hey, I called that place in Napa and got us upgraded to a villa with a hot tub. So pack whatever you'd wear in a hot tub.

GLORIA: I usually wear nothing when I'm in a hot tub.

JAY: And my college roommate's wife just had to get a new hip. Sucker.

Not to be the evil stepdad, but you put on a puffy white shirt and declare your love for a sixteen-year-old, you're gonna be swinging from the flagpole in your puffy white underwear.

GLORIA: Men need their hobbies. Manny's father had many hobbies. Like hiking in the desert, that kind of skiing that they drop you from the . . . How do you say in English?

JAY: Helicopter.

GLORIA: Yes. Once, on a dare, he even boxed with an alligator.

JAY: Wrestle. You wrestle . . . You can't box with alligators.

GLORIA: Are you sure?

JAY: How would they get gloves on those little . . . claws?

GLORIA: Aren't they like tiny little hands?

JAY: No! Okay, now I forgot what we're talking about.

I'm sorry, but there's only two places anyone should wear ponchos: Niagara Falls and log rides.

I took the heat on the bird and it was a big mistake. To this day Mitchell looks at me, I see him thinking that's the guy who killed Fliza Minnelli.

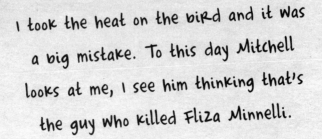

GLORIA: I'm gonna take a shower. Do you care to join me?

JAY: You know, honey, there's a gun in the footlocker in the garage. If I ever say no to that question, I want you to use it on me.

MANNY: Is Haley still coming?

JAY: You're related. I will spray you with the hose.

MITCHELL: Still keeping the traditions alive, huh?

JAY: Well, someone has to. I got two Colombians at home trying to turn Christmas into Cinco de Mayo.

MITCHELL: You know that's Mexican, right?

JAY: Eh, burrito, bur-right-o.

She's my daughter. You're my wife.
Let's remember what's important here:
There's a football game on.

DEDE: To the bride and the groom. My ex. Thirty-five years we were together and he couldn't wait ten minutes to run off with Charo. That's a joke. Seriously, I knew they were perfect when I saw his wallet and her boobs . . . Take your hands off of me!

JAY: Let me ask you something. Your sister said
that Gloria would never go for anybody who looked
like me. Now you guys basically are like women.
You know, you look . . . you look at guys. So what
do you think?

MITCHELL: You're seriously asking us if . . . if you're attractive?

JAY: Well, I know I'm no Erik Estrada or anything. I'm just curious—

MITCHELL: Dad.

JAY: So if I was in one of your bars, and the Righteous Brothers were on, you know, would you . . . uh, I don't know . . . check me out?

MITCHELL: Dad, you're really close to ruining gay for me.

JAY: Gah . . . what the hell was that!

CAMERON: Our butts pressed against each other.

JAY: They didn't press! It was glancing. Stop talking about it!

CAMERON: Oh, come on. All the time you've spent in locker rooms, this can't be your first moon landing.

JAY: You got a name for it?

CAMERON: It's very common. You got off easy. At least it didn't happen after a shower.

JAY: Enough.

CAMERON: We call that a splashdown.

Winning feels pretty great. There's nothing like that golden moment in the sun. I think every parent probably wants that for their child. And maybe a little bit for ourselves, too. Sometimes we push them too hard. And that leads to a lot of resentment and guilt. So, how much is too much? Here's where I come out . . . Guilt fades. Hardware is forever.

Gloria and I are from different generations. And I won't lie; it isn't always easy. I mean, last week she thought Simon & Garfunkel were my lawyers.

To tell you the truth, that call from my brother scared the hell out of me. I decided to get in better shape quick. I didn't wanna end up like my old man, although he did die doing what he loved: Refusing service to hippies who came into his store.

MITCHELL: Hey, uh, Dad, do you remember when I was, uh, probably eleven and you were teaching me how to fight and then I quit?

JAY: Yeah, when you said everything you needed to learn you'd learned from *West Side Story*. How'd that work out for you?

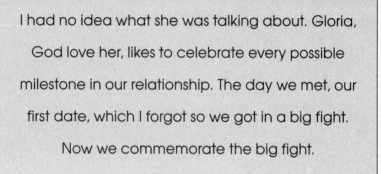

I had no idea what she was talking about. Gloria, God love her, likes to celebrate every possible milestone in our relationship. The day we met, our first date, which I forgot so we got in a big fight. Now we commemorate the big fight.

MANNY: Can I go golfing with you?

JAY: I'm probably gonna have a Latino kid carry my clubs anyway. Might as well be you.

No, he's got to learn to sell. This is
the best business training there is.
Hell, the best life training. Manny,
write this down: A good salesman goes
after Moby-Dick in a rowboat and
brings the tartar sauce with him.

JAY: Aw, jeez, why can't we eat regular food like normal people?

GLORIA: I told you, Jay. My grandmother . . . who rest in peace . . . has been coming to me in my dreams, telling me that I'm losing touch with my roots.

JAY: See, this is awkward, because my dead Uncle Joe told me to have steak tonight.

MITCHELL: Remember how much fun we had when we built that bookcase together?

JAY: That was my Vietnam. And I was in Vietnam.

I mean, it's, uh, my fault. I pushed your buttons.
My father-in-law was the same way with me.
It was horrible . . . Everything I did was wrong. If I
said it was white, he'd say it was black. Although
he'd never said anything was black because
he was a pretty big racist.

CLAIRE: Yeah, but in costume this time. You can't just show up with the backwards baseball cap and call yourself Snoop Dogg like you did last year.

JAY: I didn't even know who that guy was. Haley turned my hat around and told me to say it. I thought he was a dog detective.

JAY: What the hell is he wearing?

GLORIA: Protection pads. He needs more?

JAY: We're riding bikes; we're not training police dogs.

I'm gonna walk like a man, fast as I can, to the bar over there. And if you knew Frankie Valli, you'd be cracking up right now.

JAY: Gloria's always saying we should do more stuff together. So I agreed to watch this crazy Colombian soap opera she loves.

GLORIA: *Fuego y Hielo.*

JAY: Which apparently is Spanish for *Big Hair and Yelling.*

GLORIA: *Fire and Ice.* It's about human suffering. I relate to it.

JAY: I'm just saying the guy's a judge. He could put a shirt on.

First dance at our wedding, Gloria was all graceful and gorgeous, and I was all big and clunky, like that scene from Beauty and the Beast. Actually, that was the song. Manny picked it. He didn't like me back then.

PHIL: Thanks, Jay. Hey, look, I know you were reluctant to get that massage, but I think we can both agree it had a happy ending.

JAY: Please don't say that.

JAY: Think you better move away from that woman.

PHIL: Only we touch our women when they don't want us to.

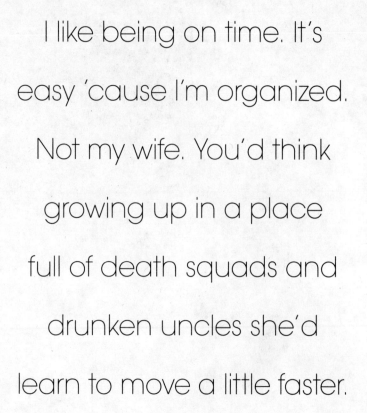

I like being on time. It's easy 'cause I'm organized. Not my wife. You'd think growing up in a place full of death squads and drunken uncles she'd learn to move a little faster.

That's how you know that your family loves you, when they feel free to scream at you . . . I guess I owe my ex-wife an apology. Apparently she was nuts about me.

JAY: Yeah, Luke did pretty good, too, for a kid that still needs help gettin' out of his backpack.

CLAIRE: Still your grandson.

JAY: I felt bad when I said it.

Gloria

In my country there's a saying that means "love is just around the corner." I come from a neighborhood with a lot of prostitutes.

I'm Colombian. I know

a fake crime scene

when I see one.

Home

What is the difference between a house and

a home?

I've never understood the difference between those two
words, so I always just say house. I don't think you need both
of these words.

In any case, I have had many houses. There is the one I
grew up in, in Colombia, which I will always remember for the
sounds of food cooking, and my sisters laughing, and the cars
in the street honking, and my mother yelling at my father to
get a better job so we could afford windows and doors.

I remember the house Javier and I brought Manny back
from the hospital to, a house that was filled with music and

dancing and five years of happiness until one day I hear the words, "I have met an American woman and I am in love." It was Manny talking about his kindergarten teacher, but soon after Javier said the same thing.

After that there was a house just for Manny and me, a small apartment we filled with pictures from Colombia and maps of places we would go. I would cut hair there at night so there was always lots of people and conversation, but still it felt a little empty.

We both knew what we needed.

A pet.

But we disagreed about what kind to get. I wanted a dog, he wanted a turtle, one day we had a big fight about it, and I went out to a restaurant by myself. Which must have been fate because I met someone that night—someone wise like a turtle, but protective like a dog—and now we live together in a new place, the most perfect house there could be. Maybe that means it's a home. Well, not yet, because it's a little cold and I don't like all his music, but we change one thing at a time. ■

CAMERON: You pierced her ears!

GLORIA: What I said. I was going to make her pretty with earrings.

MITCHELL: I thought you said "hair rings."

GLORIA: What are hair rings?

CAMERON: Yes, Mitchell, what are hair rings?

MITCHELL: Something that would tie your hair back. She said it.

GLORIA: I didn't say hair rings. I said "hair-rings." You don't like it?

CAMERON: Of course not. You punctured our daughter.

GLORIA: But did you see both sides? I didn't just do the gay ear. Look.

GLORIA: Break the flute.

JAY: What?

GLORIA: The poncho by itself, is fine. The poncho, plus the flute, plus the stupid dance . . . my son will die a virgin.

In Colombia, Manny went to Pablo Escobar Elementary School. If you were pulled out of class, it was definitely to identify a body.

> You're so funny. I'm gonna share that one with my next husband when we're spending all your money.

I always wanted a daughter . . . to dress her up in pretty dresses, to do her hair, her nails, her makeup. No one knows this, but for the first year of his life, I made up Manny like a girl and told everybody he was my daughter. I did it just a few times. I didn't want to mess with his head. When he found the pictures, I told him that it was his twin sister who died.

Manny, you were afraid to light the barbecue,

but now your eyebrows have grown back and

your salmon is legendary.

During my vows to my first husband,
drug dealers burst in and assassinated
the judge. This was way worse.

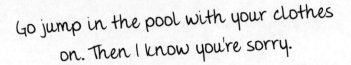
Go jump in the pool with your clothes on. Then I know you're sorry.

PETE: Ma'am, you seem to know an awful lot about sneaking contraband on to a plane.

GLORIA: Yeah, I'm Colombian.

PETE: Have you ever been to Japan?

GLORIA: I would like to make a phone call.

GLORIA: I miss babies. They never tell you to go away.

CLAIRE: Yeah, or wait in the car. I don't know about you, but I'm not gonna stand here and feel sorry for myself. You know what we should do?

GLORIA: Get pregnant.

CLAIRE: I was gonna say go for ice cream.

GLORIA: Okay. We'll do yours first.

Ai. Ai. Why the whoosh? What . . .
what did the e-mail? It sended! Ai.
Make it come back!

JAY: I'm gonna teach him real chess, not the Colombian version. We actually use the pieces to play the game, not smuggle stuff out of the country.

GLORIA: I know one Colombian piece you won't be playing with later.

I thought that one of the advantages of marrying an older guy was that I was gonna be able to relax. But all this swimming, and running, and rowing . . . it's just like how some of my relatives got into this country.

JAY: How do you . . . how do you turn the sprinklers off?

GLORIA: Ai, of course, because I'm Latina I'm supposed to know everything about gardening and sprinklers—

JAY: You were here when they installed it!

The Quinceañera is very important in the Latin culture. The moment the father dances with his little princess. I remember my own father holding my hand. There wasn't a dry eye in the cartel.

JAY: That wasn't an ambulance. I drove you.

MANNY: Then what was that siren?

JAY: That was your mother.

GLORIA: I was not that loud.

JAY: Cars pulled over, honey.

In my culture, mothers are very clingy to their sons. In fact, the leading cause of death among Colombian women is when their sons get married.

JAY: Gloria's grandfather and uncles were butchers, so she's always had a certain comfort level when it comes to . . . killing. One time, we had this rat . . .

GLORIA: What? First you just smash it, then you cut the head off.

JAY: It was like nothing to her. She left the head out there to send a message to the other rats.

GLORIA: Ai, you're not helping by protecting my feelings. I want you to be honest with me.

JAY: Okay. Well, I may have noticed some tiny little mistakes you might want to take a look at.

GLORIA: Like what?

JAY: Just little mispronunciations. Like, for example, last night you said we live in a doggy-dog world.

GLORIA: So?

JAY: It's dog-eat-dog world.

GLORIA: Well, that doesn't make any sense. Who wants to live in a world where dogs eat each other? A doggy-dog world is a beautiful world full of little puppies.

COLOMBIA

Stop my suffering! Say something terrible about me so that we are even like a Steven.

Ah, here we go. Because in Colombia we trip over goats and we kill people in the street. Do you know how offensive that is? Like we're Peruvians!

JAY: Well, hang on there. Why don't I run Claire down to the mall, and you give Phil a haircut? You're always talking about how you miss working at the salon.

GLORIA: I guess I could. I do Jay, why can't I do you?

PHIL: You can do me.

In Colombia, we couldn't go running to the hospital for every little sniffle or dislocated shoulder.

I'm not going to let Manny take off with Javier by himself. Once, when Manny was six, Javier took him to the petting zoo, which later I found out that was the name of the strippie club. A real petting zoo would have been cleaner.

GLORIA: What else do I say wrong?

JAY: Well, it's not blessings in the skies; it's blessings in disguise.

GLORIA: What else?

JAY: Carpal tunnel syndrome is not carpool tunnel syndrome—

GLORIA: And what else?

JAY: It's not volumptious—

GLORIA: Okay, enough! I know that I have an accent, but people understand me just fine!

JAY: What the hell is this?

GLORIA: I told you, Jay. I called your secretary and told her to order you a box of baby cheeses.

GLORIA: Oh, so now that is my fault, too?

GLORIA: I know how you feel. It happened to me before with another woman. And that time I was the one getting it. It hurt. I'm sorry it had to come out like this, but you have to admit that you're only happy when you're the one cracking the whip. Come on. We all know how you ride Phil. But maybe if you just let go a little, maybe even taste my cupcakes, I would join you.

CLAIRE: Uh, no. I am so confused right now.

PHIL: I may pass out.

MANNY: She can't take criticism about her driving. Once an old lady yelled at her at a crosswalk. She honked so long the horn ran out.

GLORIA: What is your report on?

MANNY: The mafia.

GLORIA: Perfect. We do a papier-mâché tommy gun.

MANNY: Oh, no, we shouldn't have to jazz it up.

GLORIA: Okay, then we go upstairs, and we get your old rocking horse, and we chop the head off.

MANNY: No, that's a terrible idea. I love Brownie!

GLORIA: Do you want to send a message or not?

Jay never wants me to help him with his business. And now suddenly, Manny doesn't want to listen to me either. It's very frustrating. I have all the answers!

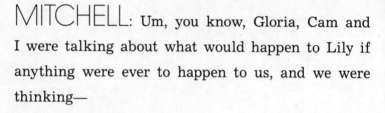

MITCHELL: Um, you know, Gloria, Cam and I were talking about what would happen to Lily if anything were ever to happen to us, and we were thinking—

GLORIA: Oh my God! Sí, sí, sí! I take her!

MITCHELL: Okay, well that's very sweet, but you realize it would only happen if—

GLORIA: I can't wait!

MITCHELL: Okay, well hopefully it's a long shot.

GLORIA: Ai, a little girl!

MITCHELL: There would have to be a very tragic accident.

GLORIA: I know. I know. Nothing is going to happen.

MITCHELL: No.

GLORIA: But if it did, we would be so happy!

JAY: And here we have . . . a phone in the shape of a mouth?

GLORIA: You're welcome! Very sexy!

JAY: Okay, wait a minute. Don't tell me. Let me work this out. I mentioned a few times I was thinking of taking up the saxophone. You give me this. I got it. Is this a sexy phone?

GLORIA: Happy birthday!

MANNY: Oh, and one time she said, "Don't choke and I'll have to do the Hindenburg maneuver."

CAMERON: Oh, one time she caught me staring off. "Oh, Cam, what's wrong? You look like a deer in head lice."

PHIL: If you tell her she doesn't have a choice, she'll say, "Don't you give me old tomato."

MITCHELL: Or when she's—

GLORIA: Okay, enough! You try talking in another language! Everybody out of my house!

Ai, please. Are you going to honestly tell me that I'm your favorite person in this family? I'm not even your favorite Colombian in this family. I would love to get closer to you. You have my number. But call me quickly, because I book up.

GLORIA: You just reminded me about my dream last night. I was in the middle of a meadow, coming down a staircase, then suddenly a black mouse showed up. He stopped, stared at me in the eyes, and opened his little mouth.

JAY: What'd it say?

GLORIA: What did he say, Jay? He was a mouse. They don't know how to talk.

JAY: Now you're playing logic police? You're standing on a staircase in a meadow?

GLORIA: In my country, when somebody dreams about a black mouse, it means that something bad is going to happen.

JAY: Ah, don't worry about it. I dreamt about a lucky blue cow. We're good to go.

JAY: Did you think that was a good idea?

GLORIA: Of course not! But I'm nice and I put on the sugar jacket.

JAY: Sugarcoating is not going to help him. He needed to hear what I said to him, even if it hurt a little bit. He's gonna thank me one day.

Maybe we are the way we are because of the people that we are with. Or maybe we just pick the people we need. However it works, when you find each other you should never let go.

Other leg. It's not marching. You're
dancing, not invading Poland.

Okay, but if this

so-called Santa Claus

doesn't bring me a

burgundy dinner jacket,

we're going to have a

big problem.

Holidays

Christmas has its tree of fir,
and gifts stacked to the ceiling.
Halloween its blood and gore,
and frights to get you squealing.

Easter all its chocolate eggs
and feast of ham and quiche.
And Valentine's, the lovers' day,
where passion's off the leash.

I love these holidays, true I do,
each one a yearly winner.
But none for me can quite compare
with the simple Sunday dinner.

For it's at these boring family times,
be they in March, June, or December
that the truest love of all does grow,
family member for family member.

Sure, some like others more at first,
but like pebbles in the sea,
our rougher sides get smoothed by time.
"Go away" becomes "sit by me."

So what do I promise in these lines,
inked on this page so gaily?
That one day I'll have a girlfriend true,
and her name will be fair Haley.

Manny Delgado

August 9, 2010

I gave her my heart and she gave me this picture of me as an old-time sheriff.

MANNY: That's her. Bianca Douglas.

GLORIA: She's so cute.

MANNY: Yeah, she has good handwriting. She's a complete package.

We're from different worlds, yet we somehow fit together. Love is what binds us, through fair or stormy weather. I stand before you now with only one agenda . . . to let you know my heart is yours, Feldman comma Brenda.

I have learned a few things in my twelve years: don't skimp on linens, don't compliment a teacher on her figure, and when it comes to my mom, never ask questions I don't want the answers to.

GLORIA: Manny, are you wearing aftershave?

MANNY: Yes. For my date. This will be the first time she will ever smell me. Her name is Whitney. I met her in an online book club. We both like vampire fiction and the romance of eternal life.

I went for the gold . . . Fiona Gunderson. I poured my heart and soul into a poem and left it on her desk. I even burned the edges to make it look fancy.

RIP Shel Turtlestein

Shel Turtlestein was many things, but, above all, he was my friend. When I didn't get a date with Fiona Gunderson, Shel was there. When I didn't get to play the part of Tevye, Shel was there. And when a raccoon broke into my room, unfortunately, Shel was there. I said a lot of things to my friend, but the one thing I never got to say was "good-bye."

MANNY: How do I look?

JAY: Like Al Capone.

MANNY: Thanks!

I noticed some lovely tweens down by the kids' club. Maybe we can find a nice spot near the pool and send over a couple of virgin mai tais. They may be interested in two sophisticated men like us.

MANNY: No. We have something in common. I'm seeing a younger woman.

JAY: How much younger are we talking about?

MANNY: Thirteen months. Her name's Chloe. She makes me feel like a fifth grader again.

I just don't understand this bad section of heaven. What if they send you to the wrong place? They make mistakes with paperwork sometimes. I was put in a girls' health class last year and had to watch a very disturbing movie.

I want to go. It's just, if I'm sick, I might get the chaperones sick, and without chaperones, it's anarchy.

GLORIA: Manny, sometimes you can be a little bit old-fashioned. Remember the first time you saw the kids with the backpacks with wheels, and you thought they were too flashy?

MANNY: You're going to school, not boarding a flight to Denver. It's getting absurd. Reuben freestyle rapped his report on Irish immigrants. That doesn't even make sense. Maybe you do *Riverdance*. Maybe.

MANNY: It's the "Bieber-ization" of America.

JAY: What do beavers have to do with anything?

GLORIA: The beavers, they build the dams all over the country, so there's no floods. It's the beaver-ization of the Americas.

MANNY: I'm finding there's less and less we can talk about.

JAY: Buddy, don't close yourself off from new things. Ever tell you the story about me and crab cakes? Thought I didn't like 'em. Tried them. Love them.

MANNY: Wow. Are the movie rights available for that one?

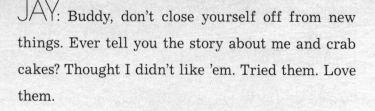

She intimidates me. Every time I open my mouth I say something stupid. I called her bathroom "fantazing." That's not even a word!

GLORIA: I want my ears to pop.

MANNY: Try putting a little rouge on 'em . . . Nobody gets me.

CAMERON: And you know what? I wouldn't worry too much. She's gonna like you even if sports aren't your thing.

MANNY: Aren't my thing? I have a tennis racket upstairs I only use as a bubble-bath frother.

MANNY: Do we book spa treatments through you or . . . ?

HANK: I like you, kid. I'm gonna call you Hollywood.

MANNY: That wasn't an answer.

MANNY: Hello, ma'am. Do you love Christmas?

NEIGHBOR: Actually, I'm Jewish.

MANNY: Well, then, you must appreciate a good value.

JAY: Oh, geez.

You'll never go broke playing to a rich guy's ego. Write that down.

The Tucker-
Pritchetts

Cam, Mitchell & Lily

CAMERON: Okay. The house is on fire. I only have time to grab one shirt . . . Which one do I take?

MITCHELL: The correct answer is: Take Lily.

CAMERON: I used to be a music teacher, but I gave that up as soon as Lily came along.

MITCHELL: Yes, we just felt that it was really important that one of us stayed home to raise her. So . . .

CAMERON: And that's not a judgment on other people's choices. It's just that we happen to be a very traditional family.

MITCHELL: Yes, that's what the disabled lesbian shaman who blessed Lily's room said too . . .

Love
by Mitchell

I was twenty-nine years old, and I had a great job at a top law firm and a chic apartment decorated just how I wanted it. I had taste and class and the rock-hard abs you can only get by doing forty sit-ups every other morning, and I looked at myself in the mirror and said, "I love it. I love my life." And I did love it.

Not long after I was at a fund-raiser playing charades and I met a man who was attractive but not too attractive, charming but not too charming—well, I don't remember exactly how he described himself, but it was something like that. Anyway, three months later we moved in together. Good-bye chic apartment, hello "Oh, you're putting that there?" But a few weeks in I found myself saying, "I love this."

And I meant it.

A few years later we were out to breakfast and in came our friends Caleb and Guy, pushing a stroller. We both caught each other staring at that stroller, and two years later *The Lion King* music played and we had Lily. And there have been first words, and dance recitals, and moments just putting tiny T-shirts in a drawer when I've found myself thinking, "I love this."

And I never meant anything more.

So was I wrong all those times before? Was I that good at deluding myself about what I need to be happy? Or do I just have one of those hearts that's a little slutty and a little greedy (why do I hear my dad saying, "Well, you are a gay lawyer"?), a heart that knows it likes to feel love and always wants to know new ways to feel it? I think it's the second, and I think we're all a little slutty that way. ∎

MITCHELL: Okay, well, this one says, "When my daughter bit her brother, I put a pinch of pepper in her mouth. She cried and cried, but she never bit again." Smiley face.

CAMERON: Oh, well, the smiley face makes it okay. "I water boarded our toddler . . . " LOL.

MITCHELL: Why is our daughter dressed like Donna Summer?

CAMERON: She is not Donna Summer. Clearly she's Diana Ross from the RCA years. . . . How is Daddy not seeing that?

Mitchell: I am losing my mind. As much as I love Lily . . . which is, you know, more than life itself . . . I am not cut out to be a stay-at-home dad. No, but it's, it's Cameron's turn . . . It's Cameron's turn to be out in the world, interacting with other grown-ups while I get to stay at home and . . . and plot the death of Dora the Explorer . . . to fill her backpack with bricks and throw her into Candy Cane River.

CAMERON: Oh, well there's your esteem-building parent right there. Wait, wait, I think I hear future Lily sending us a message from her stripper pole: "Thanks, gay dead Dads, this dance is for you."

Cameron: Excuse me. Meryl Streep could play Batman and be the right choice. She's perfection, whether she's divorcing Kramer, whether she's wearing Prada. And don't even get me started on *Sophie's Choice* . . . She couldn't forgive herself. I get emotional thinking about it . . . She couldn't forgive herself. And . . . she had to choose. And I think because now I have . . . we have . . . we have . . . we have Lily, it's so hard to imagine being put in that position. If I had to choose Lily or Mitchell, I mean I would choose Li—I don't know! I don't know! I don't know! I don't know!

MITCHELL: Okay, you know what? Yes. Alright, listen, I might still be holding a little resentment. But that's embarrassing and petty and it's not a good color on me. It's kind of like you and yellow.

CAMERON: You love me in my yellow shirt.

MITCHELL: It makes you look like the sun.

CAMERON: Bubbling. Hurtful bubbling.

CAMERON: Sal is our very best friend in the whole wide world. The reason we love her so much is she has absolutely no inhibitions.

MITCHELL: No.

CAMERON: And that's before she starts drinking. Hanging out with her is like an Amsterdam Saturday night every day of the week.

MITCHELL: And ironically, Sal's not allowed back into Amsterdam.

CAMERON: Any day of the week

SAL: You should kill the baby.

MITCHELL: What?

SAL: You should call the baby. I love you guys so much!

CAMERON: Did she just—

MITCHELL: I'm scared.

CAMERON: Look at those queens. I would have killed with this crowd. But you had to clip my wings. Which, you used to be the wind beneath.

CAMERON: I've known I wanted to be a clown since I found out clowns were just people with makeup.

CAMERON [*British accent*]: Sir Fizbo-lot, royal court jester, at your service. I understand there's a little princess 'oos in need of a jolly good time.

MITCHELL: No.

CAMERON [*British accent*]: Your 'ighness said a clown doesn't fit the princess theme, but mefinks that a court jester is right as rain.

CAMERON: The new Greensleevers. Is there a slap mark on my face? I mean, why is Edna singing the low harmony? It's like people are applauding out of shock.

■

CAMERON: There's something wrong with you that the sound of our child in such distress doesn't bother you more.

MITCHELL: She's not in distress and this just proves that you need this more than she does. I'm Ferberizing two babies.

CAMERON: Raccoons slipped into the Lawsons' home and stole a loaf of bread.

MITCHELL: Your point?

CAMERON: That we left Lily's window open a crack, and those raccoons need something to put between that bread, and that is Lily. I'm coming for you, Lily!

CAMERON: Redheaded Daddy is angry Daddy.

Mitchell: Listen, Cam, I . . . I can't always be the bad cop here. I know it's my issue, but she can't grow up with one huggy, happy, cuddly dad and one frowny, lesson-teachy dad. Because guess which one she's gonna ask to walk her down the aisle.

CAMERON: Yes, I'm a caring person. And without Mitchell I would just keep giving and giving and giving. I'm like a big runaway charity truck and Mitchell is my off-ramp full of safety gravel. He knows how to say no. He always can put himself first. He certainly can turn his back on someone suffering. Um—

MITCHELL: No really, keep going . . .

CAMERON: He—

MITCHELL: Don't keep going.

MITCHELL: Hey Cam, does the gardener usually work on Saturdays?

CAMERON: I don't know. He comes when we need him. He's like Batman but straight.

CAMERON: Okay, I speak a little Spanish. Señor, te gustaria hacer el agua y tenemos nuestra cama? [*Subtitle: Sir, would you like to make water and have our bed?*]

Mitchell: I came out of the closet in my midtwenties. I had to actually come out to my dad three times before he finally acknowledged it. I'm not sure if maybe he was hoping he heard it wrong. Like I had said, "Dad, I'm gray."

MITCHELL: I'm . . . I'm proud of you, Dad. And you're growing.

JAY: Just, just stop it. Please. Don't you see how hard this is for me? See, I used to be just like one of those guys. Now look at me. I got a house that looks like little Colombia. I've got a gay son, and a Chinese granddaughter—

MITCHELL: Vietnamese.

JAY: Only you would know the difference.

MITCHELL: Don't worry, Dad, not growing too much.

Cameron: Mitchell's mother has a problem with me. Last Christmas, for example, she gave me a piece of exercise equipment and a lettuce dryer. So, to recap, I gave her a gorgeous pair of diamond earrings, and she gave me a hint.

CAMERON: When Mitchell was ten—

MITCHELL: Eleven.

CAMERON: And Claire was thirteen, they were competitive ice dancers—

MITCHELL: Figure skaters! Oh, for god's sakes I'll tell the story. Yes, my sister and I were actually a very good team. We were called "Fire and Nice." I was "Fire," because of the red hair, and Claire was "Nice," because it was ironic and she wasn't.

CAMERON: And Mitchell is still upset because Claire quit the team right before some meet.

MITCHELL: Some meet. The thirteen and under regional championships. Just the Emerald City at the end of my yellow brick road.

CAMERON: Wow. You did it.

MITCHELL: What?

CAMERON: You made figure skating sound even gayer.

JAY: Uh, it looks like I gotta watch the game with Dick Butkus.

MITCHELL: Dad! Dad, come on. That's offensive.

CAMERON: No, Mitchell, he's one of the greatest linebackers to ever play at Illinois, and one of my personal heroes.

MITCHELL: And his name is Butkus. And we're just choosing to . . . okay . . . alright. I'm sorry, Dad. I thought you were being homophobic. I'm sorry.

CAMERON: Well, Mitchell is an amazing lawyer. My dream for him is that one day he'll be on the Supreme Court.

MITCHELL: Why, Cam?

CAMERON: So at parties I could tell everyone my partner is one of the Supremes.

CAMERON: I'm taking the negative charge out of the word "adopted." [To Lily] Yay!

MITCHELL: What did Oprah do now?

CAMERON: Well, she had on a girl who at sixteen found out that she was adopted. And felt betrayed, and ran away, and became a stripper. And not the heart-of-gold kind, the by-the-airport kind.

MITCHELL: Okay.

CAMERON: Alright, go get your gavel, Judge Judy.

MITCHELL: No, not at all. I'm adopting [to Lily] yay! A tolerant attitude towards your flights of lunacy.

Mitchell: Take it down a notch. We're trying to make a friend, not initiate a three-way

MITCHELL: Well, her first word was every gay father's worst nightmare.

CAMERON: Mommy.

CAMERON: You know, it's because you're Asian, right?

MITCHELL: Cam . . .

CAMERON: No, I'm sorry. What? Am I just supposed to ignore the giant panda in the room?

DR. MIURA: Pandas are from China. I'm . . . well, it doesn't matter.

MITCHELL: Okay, okay. Um, I think what my hysterical partner is just trying to say is . . . And if I may, that for the first six months of her life, Lily was raised by very loving Asian women in the orphanage with whom she clearly bonded and then suddenly you come in with your Asian-ness and, and your breasts, and womb, and lady bits, and it all just comes rushing back to her . . .

MITCHELL: Did you pack, the, uh, bread for the ducks?

CAMERON: Yes.

MITCHELL: Not the whole wheat kind, the ducks don't like that.

CAMERON: They're ducks, Mitchell. They don't care.

Cameron: There's a fish in nature that swims around with its babies in its mouth. That fish would look at Mitchell's relationship with his mother and say, "That's messed up."

Cameron: When Mitchell and I first met, I may have exaggerated my interest in adventurous travel . . . by implying that I had any. But it's one of the things he loves most about me, and I can't tell him the truth now. It would be like Lewis telling Clark that he didn't like to walk. Side note, we're very good friends with a couple named Lewis and Clark. Clark bought a big sparkly belt in New Orleans that he calls his Louisiana purchase.

MITCHELL: Oh, please. Where was all this conscience when I got us into the first-class lounge at the airport and you chewed Angela Lansbury's ear off? You know what you are? You're like a mob wife. You look down at me and my ways, but you're happy to wear the mink coat that fell off the back of the truck.

Cameron: Mitchell has a problem with public displays of affection. Um, I remember once at a New Year's Eve party, stroke of midnight, he high-fived me. Two problems with that: One, gays don't high-five. Two, gays don't high-five.

CAMERON [*as if reading a children's book*]: While the spray-tanned starlet claims to be six weeks sober, sources down under say she has been barhopping like a coked-up kangaroo.

MITCHELL: Ah, what's Daddy reading to you?

CAMERON: If I have to read *The Very Hungry Caterpillar* one more time, I will snap.

Mitchell: My great-great-grandfather helped build the Brooklyn Bridge. And I heard that until the day he died, every time he passed it, he was filled with such pride. He'd say, "There's a little bit of me in that bridge." I know that I'm not the handiest guy, but I'm still a man. And I want to be able to look out in my yard and say, "There's a little bit of me in that princess castle."

Cameron: If an accident does happen, I hope he kills me, because I don't think I would be a very inspiring disabled person.

■

CAMERON: Mitchell, I get scared. When you're around tools, honey, it's dangerous. For me, for you, for our roses.

MITCHELL: Do you know how insulting this is? I was an intern at the Songbird Summer Playhouse. Do you think that the town of Brigadoon just magically appeared? Well, in the play, it did. But the set, the set was built with these two hands.

■

Cameron: Because I can assure you if our child did something like this, we would be on her like white on rice. And I know that sounds a little bit like a racial slur because we're white and she presumably likes rice, but I didn't intend it that way.

Mitchell: This is perfect. Leave it to the gays to raise the only underachieving Asian in America.

■

CAMERON: Oh. We should also mention how she always perks up when we watch *Charlie Rose*.

MITCHELL: That was one time. He was interviewing Elmo.

■

MITCHELL: Cam, this is the first time that being gay is a competitive advantage. They're choosing a team for gym class and we're finally getting picked first.

CAMERON: I always got picked first. I could throw a dodge ball through a piece of plywood. But I see your point.

CAMERON: Disabled interracial lesbians with an African kicker.

MITCHELL: Did not see that coming.

CAMERON: The tribe elders foretold that though I lay with fire-haired man, the giving hawk would bring us baby. With her skin the color of sweet corn . . . which my people call maize.

MITCHELL: Please stop.

MR. PLYMPTON: Well, uh . . .

CAMERON: Knowledge is her sustenance, like so much maize . . . which, you'll remember, means corn.

MITCHELL: What if I were a single dad?

CAMERON: Well, I don't want to overstate this, but my mom is the greatest woman that ever lived.

MITCHELL: Cam loves his mom.

CAMERON: She raised four kids, two barns, and a whole lotta hell.

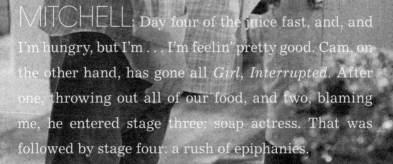

MITCHELL: Day four of the juice fast, and, and I'm hungry, but I'm . . . I'm feelin' pretty good. Cam, on the other hand, has gone all *Girl, Interrupted*. After one, throwing out all of our food, and two, blaming me, he entered stage three: soap actress. That was followed by stage four: a rush of epiphanies.

CAMERON: I . . . don't . . . need . . . food. Look at this. Architecture is everywhere. Spaniards make amazing athletes.

MITCHELL: Into stage five: despair.

LILY: Daddy, we hided, but you didn't seek.

MITCHELL: What?

CAMERON: You know what I'm looking for.

MITCHELL: He's a very nice guy.

CAMERON: That's not it.

MITCHELL: I'm sorry I made a snap judgment.

CAMERON: Still not it.

MITCHELL: You were right.

CAMERON: There she is.

CAMERON: I knew this would happen! Why do you have to throw a wet blanket on my dreams?

MITCHELL: I do not.

CAMERON: You do it all the time! And you know what I end up with? Wet dreams . . . I heard it as soon as I said it. Just leave it alone.

Mitchell: Did you not hear her on the phone? "Fix it, replace it, write me a check!" She probably has that embroidered on a pillow, right next to a jar of human tears.

"People Aren't Food"
by Cam Tucker

Take a bite of an apple. Take a bite of a pear.

Take a bite of the cookie that you left over there.

Here's one thing you should never ever do:

Don't bite Taylor or Brandon or Sue.

People aren't food. People aren't food.

Your friends will run away if they're scared of being chewed.

And as a side note, private parts are private.

TWO MONKEYS & A PANDA

Once upon a time, there were two monkeys. They loved each other very much, but there was something missing. They wanted a baby. And they heard that there was a very special baby in a faraway land who needed a family. She was a panda named Lily. One of the monkeys was scared. They'd never had a panda before. But then they held Lily in their arms and the scared monkey became the brave one. And the two monkeys, Coco and Miko, traveled all the way home with the perfect panda that they adopted.

CAMERON: Well, I had no idea. I had no idea I was surrounded by a bunch of quitters. This production was a joke until I introduced these children to the musical theater greats: Bernstein, Sondheim. Years from now, some of these kids will still be talking about the way I Sondheim-ized them.

MITCHELL: Oh, I don't think that's a good way of saying it.

Cameron: Where's the *L*? Where's the *L*?!

MITCHELL: Saturday night we're having dinner with Pepper, Longinus, and Crispin.

CAMERON: They're our gay friends.

MITCHELL: I think that was clear.

MITCHELL: Well, you know what? We needed a sitter. She's family. I say we give her a shot.

CAMERON: A shot! Oh, with our only child? Sure, why not? If something goes wrong we'll just pop over to the Orient and grab another one.

CAMERON: There's nothing gays hate more than when people treat us . . .

CAMERON/MITCHELL: Like we're women.

CAMERON: We're not. We don't wanna go to your baby shower. We don't have a time of the month. We don't love pink.

MITCHELL: You love pink.

CAMERON: No, pink loves me.

MITCHELL: Okay, well . . .

Cameron (*reading from an old yearbook*): "You're the cutest boy in school. We're gonna have an awesome summer. Smooches, Brenda." Oh, Brenda, you're about to have the most confusing summer of your life.

CAMERON: Look at us. I can snap you like a twig.

MITCHELL: Okay, every once in a while you say that thing about the twig, and I need you to know that it bothers me.

Mitchell: God forbid I say anything negative about his mom. One time I added salt to her casserole . . . and he went into the garage and punched the car.

Cameron: Show me, Mitchell. Show me on Lily's doll where my mother is touching you.

MITCHELL: We are having a slight issue getting Lily on board with the adoption. "I hate the baby."

CAMERON: "No new baby."

MITCHELL: "I want to make the baby dead."

CAMERON: I thought we weren't going to share that one.

Cameron (*into cell phone*): Hello. Oh, Mitchell, you are not going to believe this. I'm out helping Gloria look for her dog. I'm wearing an undershirt, and I'm screaming "Stella," just like in *Streetcar*.

CAMERON: Uh, excuse me. Hi, sweetie. What's your name?

BLANCHE: Blanche.

CAMERON: Shut up. Mitchell would die. Listen, we don't know you. You seem like a very sweet little girl, and right now we're forced to . . . I can't believe I'm saying this to you . . . rely on the kindness of strangers.

MITCHELL: So we haven't told the family yet, but we've decided to adopt a baby boy.

CAMERON: From America this time. You might say we're buying domestic.

MITCHELL: In private. You might say that in private.

CAMERON: This award has changed you, Mitchell. You may be flying high now, but pretty soon you're gonna be free-fallin', Tom Petty. Because you're petty. Tom Petty. Hmm? Get it?

MITCHELL: About three sentences ago.

Mitchell: Claire is the son that my dad never had. I mean, he just wanted someone who'd throw a ball in the backyard. I did once, but he did not attend.

You'd think the dreamers would find the dreamers and the realists would find the realists . . . but more often than not, the opposite is true.

The following writers contributed to the wit and wisdom of *Modern Family* (listed in alphabetical order):

Cindy Chupak

Jerry Collins

Paul Corrigan

Sameer Asad Gardezi

Abraham Higginbotham

Ben Karlin

Elaine Ko

Joe Lawson

Carol Leifer

Steven Levitan

Christopher Lloyd

Dan O'Shannon

Jeffrey Richman

Brad Walsh

Ilana Wernick

Caroline Williams

Bill Wrubel

Danny Zuker

Writers Assistants:

Bianca Douglas

Clint McCray